This Ladybird Book belongs to:

_____

_____

_____

_____

All children
have a great ambition …
to read by themselves.

Through traditional and popular stories, each title
in the **Read It Yourself** series introduces children to
the most commonly used words in the English
language (*Key Words*), plus additional words
necessary to tell the story.
The additional words appearing in this book are
listed below.

Country, Mouse, Town, quiet,
owl, catch, supper, food, sleep, buy, park,
carpet, cleaner, hole, Christmas, present

Ladybird books are widely available, but in case of
difficulty may be ordered by post or telephone from:

Ladybird Books – Cash Sales Department
Littlegate Road Paignton Devon TQ3 3BE
Telephone 0803 554761

A catalogue record for this book is available
from the British Library

Published by Ladybird Books Ltd Loughborough Leicestershire UK
Ladybird Books Inc Auburn Maine 04210 USA

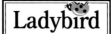

Town Mouse
and
Country Mouse

retold by Alison Ainsworth
illustrated by John Dyke

This is Country Mouse.

Country Mouse lives in
the country.

He has a home in a big tree.

Here is Town Mouse.

Town Mouse lives in the town.

He has a home
in a town house.

Town Mouse goes to stay
in the country.
Country Mouse says,
"I like it here. It is quiet.

"Stay with me here, Town Mouse, and we can have fun," he says.

This owl comes down to catch
Town Mouse.

Town Mouse and
Country Mouse run away.

Country Mouse says,
"Look! Town Mouse,
come into my house."

Country Mouse and
Town Mouse have supper.

Town Mouse says, "I don't like the food in the country. It is not like the food in the town."

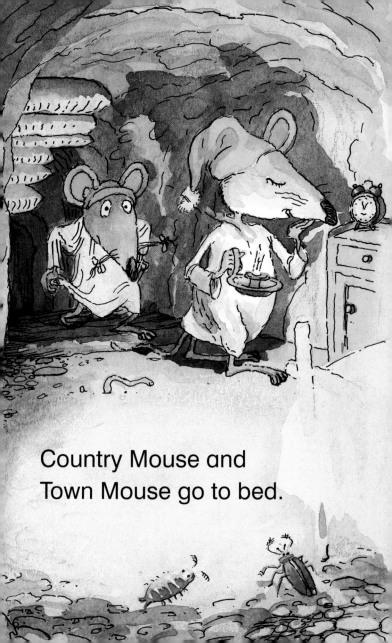

Country Mouse and
Town Mouse go to bed.

Town Mouse says, "I don't like this bed.

"It's not like my bed in the town."

Town Mouse says to Country Mouse, "It's too quiet in the country.

"I can't go to sleep."

Country Mouse has to look
for some food.

He says to Town Mouse,
"Come with me and look
for some food!"

Town Mouse says, "No!
I don't want to look for food.
In the town we have shops.
We can buy food."

Some horses come to see
Town Mouse and
Country Mouse.

Town Mouse runs away.
He jumps into the water.

Town Mouse says, "I don't like the country.

"In the town it's not like this.
We don't have horses.
We have shops in the town.

"Come and stay in the town
with me, Country Mouse.
You can have supper and go
to the shops in the town."

Town Mouse sees a man
with a car.

"Look, Country Mouse,"
he says, "we can go
to the town in this car."

They jump into the car.

The car goes to the town.

Country Mouse sees
lots of shops.

He sees all the cars.

It's not quiet in the town!

Town Mouse says, "I like the town.

"My home is not in a tree. I live in a town house.

"Stay here with me,
Country Mouse,
and we can have fun."

Town Mouse and
Country Mouse have supper.

se and
ouse go
k.

use has a ball.
y with it.

Country Mouse says, "I don't
like the food in the town.

"It's not like the food
in the country."

Town Mouse and
Country Mouse go to bed.

Co...
"I d...
like r...
It's no...
I can't...

Town Mou...
Country M...
to the pa...

Town Mo...
They pla...

A dog comes for the ball.
Country Mouse runs away.

He jumps into the water.

In the town house,
Country Mouse sees
a carpet cleaner.

He runs away.

Town Mouse says, "Here!
Country Mouse, come
into the hole with me."

A cat comes to catch
Town Mouse and
Country Mouse.

They are in the hole.
They have no food.

Country Mouse says, "I don't like cats. I want to go home to the country. It's quiet there."

Country Mouse sees
a Christmas tree
and some presents.

"Look!" says Town Mouse,
"This present is going
to the country.

"You can go home in it."
The man puts the present in
the car. Country Mouse is
in the present. The car takes
Country Mouse home.

Country Mouse says, "Here is my home in the tree."

He says, "I don't like the town. It's not quiet.

Country Mouse says, "I don't like the food in the town.

"It's not like the food in the country."

Town Mouse and
Country Mouse go to bed.

Country Mouse says,
"I don't like this bed. It's not
like my bed in the country.
It's not quiet here.
I can't sleep."

Town Mouse and
Country Mouse go
to the park.

Town Mouse has a ball.
They play with it.

"I am a Country Mouse and this is my home. I like it here."

WITHDRAWN

Support material available: Practice Books, Double Cassette pack,
Flash Cards